KU-541-539

Knight Time

Jane Clarke and Jane Massey

RED FOX

In the time of the knights,

it was (k)night time again.

Little Knight and Little Drago

Their daddies re
them a sto

...ere getting ready for bed.

...ked them into bed
...d kissed them
...odnight.

And then their daddies went out.

It was a night for nightmares
and things that go **bump** in the night.

Little Knight was
sure the dragon
was going to
eat him!

Their rooms were full of **scary shadows**.

Little Dragon was sure the knight was going to eat him!

"I want my daddy!"

hey cried.

ut their daddies were in the forest,
and the forest was **very dark**
and **very,**
very . . .

Will their daddies hear their cries?
Will their daddies come to save them?

Yes! Their daddies held them tight.

But . . .

Do knights have scales?

Do dragons wear armour?

NO!

"Please don't eat me!" Little Knight
and Little Dragon cried, at the very same time.

"I don't eat knights," said **Daddy Dragon**.

"I don't eat dragons," said Daddy Knight.

"Then why do dragons hunt knights,
and knights hunt dragons?"
the little ones asked.

"Because they're **VERY SCARY!**" said
their daddies, at the very same time.

Little Knight looked at Little Dragon's
teddy bear and blanket.
"You're not **that scary!**" he said.

Little Dragon looked at Little Knight's teddy bear and blanket.
"You're not that scary, either!" he said.

"Then it's silly to hunt each other,"
Little Knight and Little Dragon told their daddies.

"But we always hunt each other at this time of night," their daddies wailed. "Whatever are we going to do?"

"You could try to be friends," said
Little Knight and Little Dragon, "like us!"

So from then on,

the time of the knights was a lot more fun . . .

. . . and (k)night time was lovely and peaceful.

Sweet dreams, everyone!

For Dennis – JC
For the Trevor Mann Baby Unit and RSCH, Brighton – JM

KNIGHT TIME
A RED FOX BOOK 978 1 849 41804 1

First published in Great Britain by Red Fox, an imprint of Random House Children's Publishers UK
A Random House Group Company

Red Fox edition published 2008
This edition published 2012

1 3 5 7 9 10 8 6 4 2

Text copyright © Jane Clarke, 2008
Illustrations copyright © Jane Massey, 2008

The right of Jane Clarke and Jane Massey to be identified as the author and illustrator
of this work has been asserted in accordance with the Copyright, Designs and Patents Act 1988.

All rights reserved. No part of this publication may be reproduced, stored in a retrieval system, or transmitted in any form
or by any means, electronic, mechanical, photocopying, recording or otherwise, without the prior permission of the publishers.

RANDOM HOUSE CHILDREN'S PUBLISHERS UK
61–63 Uxbridge Road, London W5 5SA

www.randomhousechildrens.co.uk   www.randomhouse.co.uk

Addresses for companies within The Random House Group Limited can be found at: www.randomhouse.co.uk/offices.htm

THE RANDOM HOUSE GROUP Limited Reg. No. 954009

A CIP catalogue record for this book is available from the British Library.

Printed in China